More Than Words:

A Book About Body Language

By Amy Jivani

Huskies Pub

Text © 2020 Amy Jivani
Cover and Interior Art © 2020 Amy Jivani

More Than Words- A Book About Body Language

Library of Congress Control Number: 2020939364

First Edition
ISBN
Hardcover: 978-1-64372-144-6
Softcover: 978-1-64372-141-5

For orders, visit
www.huskiespub.com

It's hard to hear how people feel,
When there are no words to make it real.

But there is a way without a word
how someone's feelings can be heard.

Body language helps me out
in case there are no words to shout.
It gives me clues on what to do
and helps me feel along with you!

What body language do I see?
What emotion could that be?

...Happy!
I see a smiling mouth!
I see raised cheeks!
I see open eyes!
Can you make a happy face?

Body language helps me out
in case there are no words to shout.
It gives me clues on what to do
and helps me feel along with you!

What body language do I see?
What emotion could that be?

...Angry!
I see crossed arms!
I see nostrils flaring!
I see lowered eyebrows!
Can you make an angry face?

Body language helps me out in
case there are no words to shout.
It gives me clues on what to do
and helps me feel along with you!

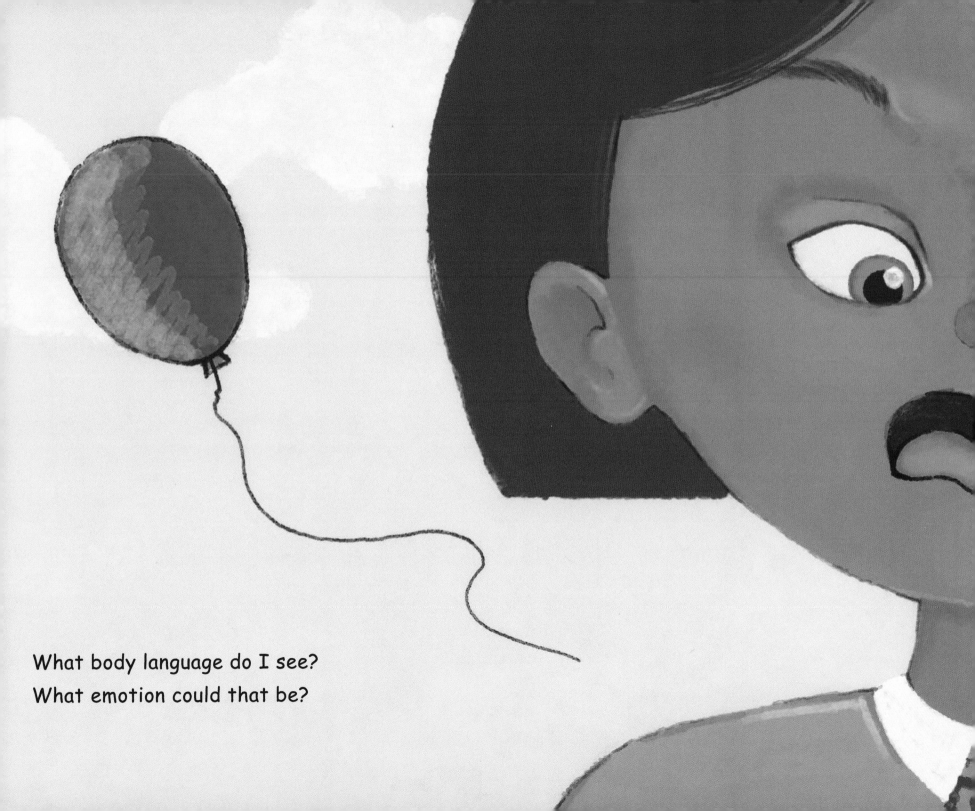

What body language do I see?
What emotion could that be?

...Disgusted!
I see a wrinkled nose!
I see a tongue sticking out!
I see narrowing eyes!
Can you make a disgusted face?

Body language helps me out
in case there are no words to shout.
It gives me clues on what to do
and helps me feel along with you!

What body language do I see?
What emotion could that be?

...Sad!
I see a frowning mouth!
I see drooping eyes!
I see hunched shoulders!
Can you make a sad face?

Body language helps me out
in case there are no words to shout.
It gives me clues on what to do
and helps me feel along with you!

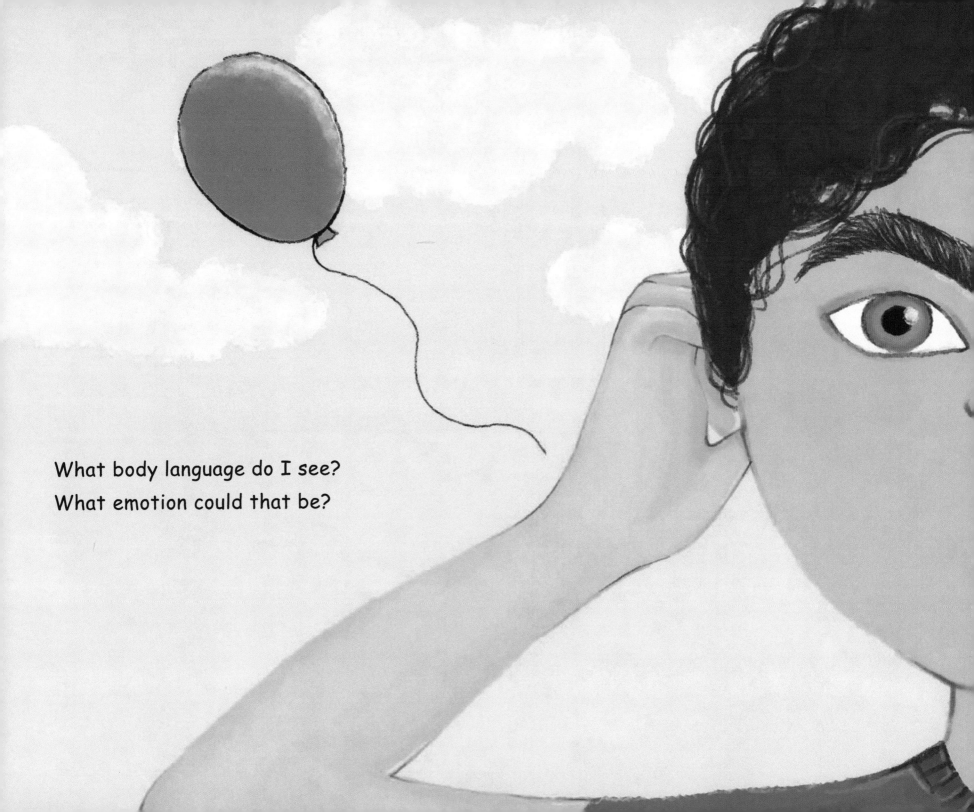

What body language do I see?
What emotion could that be?

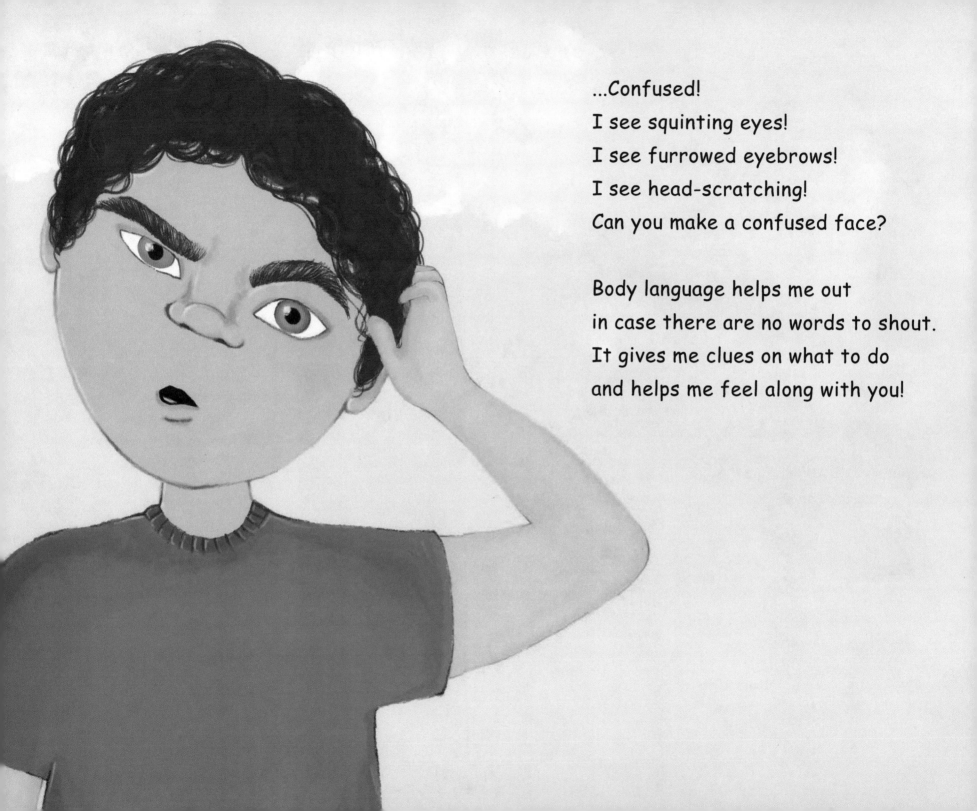

...Confused!
I see squinting eyes!
I see furrowed eyebrows!
I see head-scratching!
Can you make a confused face?

Body language helps me out
in case there are no words to shout.
It gives me clues on what to do
and helps me feel along with you!

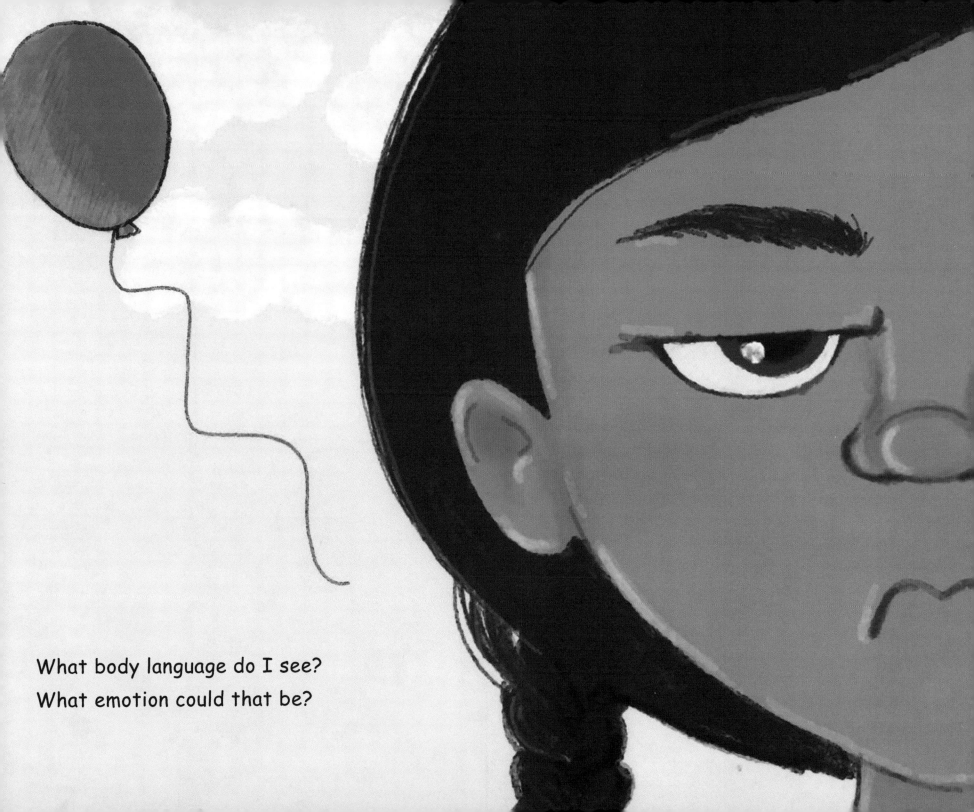

What body language do I see?
What emotion could that be?

...Annoyed!
I see folded arms!
I see eyes rolling!
I see lips curled!
Can you make an annoyed face?

Body language helps me out
in case there are no words to shout.
It gives me clues on what to do
and helps me feel along with you!

What body language do I see?
What emotion could that be?

...Surprised!
I see an open mouth!
I see raised eyebrows!
I see wide eyes!
Can you make a surprised face?

Body language helps me out
in case there are no words to shout.
It gives me clues on what to do
and helps me feel along with you!

What body language do I see?
What emotion could that be?

...Embarrassed!
I see blushing cheeks!
I see a bowing head!
I see eyes looking down!
Can you make an embarrassed face?

Body language helps me out
in case there are no words to shout.
It gives me clues on what to do
and helps me feel along with you!

So when there are no words to shout,
Body language helps me out!
Now I know just what to do,
To understand your feelings too!

Amy Jivani
Author-Illustrator

Amy is a 1st-grade teacher living in Denton, Texas.
When she is not teaching and coming up with stories, she loves to
spend time outdoors with her husband, Arman, her son, Rain, and
Juno the Schipperke.

CPSIA information can be obtained at www.ICGtesting.com
Printed in the USA
BVIW120600200720
583894BV00001B/9